OBSESSION

G. V.

ALSO BY GLORIA VANDERBILT

It Seemed Important at the Time

A Mother's Story

The Memory Book of Starr Faithful

Never Say Goodbye

Black Knight, White Knight

Once Upon a Time

Love Poems

GLORIA

OBSESSION

VANDERBILT

AN EROTIC TALE

ECCO

For information, address HarperCollins Publishers,

10 East 53rd Street, New York, NY 10022.

HarperCollins books may be purchased for educational,

business, or sales promotional use.

For information, please write:

Special Markets Department, HarperCollins Publishers,

10 East 53rd Street, New York, NY 10022.

FIRST EDITION

Designed by Chip Kidd

Photography by Geoff Spear

Library of Congress Cataloging-in-Publication Data
Vanderbilt, Gloria
    Obsession / Gloria Vanderbilt. — 1st ed.
        p. cm.
ISBN: 978-0-06-173489-2
I. Title.
PS3572.A42828O37   2009
813'.54—dc22   2008036948

09 10 11 12 13   OV/RRD   10 9 8 7 6 5 4 3

DEDICATED
TO Q.

ACKNOWLEDGMENTS

My thanks to Daniel Halpern for the brilliance of his vision.
To Chip Kidd—as ever, endless admiration.
To Jeannette Watson for her friendship and encouragement.
To Helene Goulay and the Corner Bookstore for unfailing support.
To Jeanne Carter, agent supreme.
To the team at Ecco-HarperCollins for their involvement and commitment.

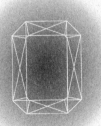

OBSESSION

IF EVER TWO WERE ONE, it could be said of Priscilla and Talbot Bingham. How charmed Priscilla would be to hear the couple described in this Victorian manner, conjuring up old-fashioned valentines with quaint phrases entwined by ribbons and hearts, bordered by paper lace. For to her, image was all: childless by choice, proud to devote her life "constructing," as her architect husband might say, "brick by brick," the castle—high topped by a banner proclaiming to the world the success of their partnership.

Guests would agree—if ever two were one, it was the Binghams—as they toasted the couple at the country club on the eastern shore of Maryland—and watched Priscilla disintegrate after Talbot died of a heart attack in the middle of their tenth wedding anniversary celebration. It was terrible to see—the stretcher carrying Talbot's body away—Priscilla on a stretcher in the ambulance as though she too had died.

But she hadn't. All she did was live with her grief and after a time found herself walking and talking once again like a normal person. Nobody would have suspected that when she looked in a mirror, the eyes of a dead person stared back. Gone, lost and gone forever, dreadful sorry Clementine, she would sing to herself and cry as if tears came from a well high in the mountains. The cold, cold mountains where nothing grew, no creature lived, nothing except intermittent snow falling and winds releasing avalanches that fell upon her heart, suffocating.

I HAD MET TALBOT at a dance over Christmas vacation when I was a senior at Miss Porter's School in Farmington, Connecticut. He had already graduated from Harvard and was on his way to being America's most controversial architect. Although not handsome, he had the grace and movement of an athlete. There was something indefinable about him, brilliant and complex bursting with supercharged yet strangely childlike energy combined with an inherent dilemma which belongs to the coexistence of two trends, often a defect of artists of all kinds—the urgent need to communicate and the still more urgent need not to be found. All part of the fascination and mystery about him, a puzzle; women flirted with the notion that only they might find the missing piece. But not a chance. His devotion to me was beyond question and those who attempted soon gave up, stepping back into mutual friendship with "the Talbots." I adored everything about him, from his half-curling rough black hair, accentuating black olive eyes capable of expressing every emotion of his animated mind, inherited from his Roman mother, to his contradictory withdrawn silences and eccentricities, a maze of paradoxes I decided early on to leave unresolved. Obsessively secretive in his relationships, even with me, he remained an enigma to the

4

world and to his closest friends. Of course, he was a genius. But that particular magic I loved most about him was that from our first meeting he had been passionate in his possession of my skinny body, which in my mind lacked a femininity I thought essential and admired in other women. After ten years, he still, when he returned home after a trip, greeted me at the door and always demanded to make love, instantly, before even taking off his coat. This intensity never failed to be a jolt of lightning that transformed my insecurities into an image of myself I was proud of, pushing away the knowledge that I was an impostor who in truth found sex of little interest. But no matter—it triggered passion in the man I admired and loved, and without being aware of it I slipped into a lie of pretense, acting, performing as if I too felt passion as he did. But that was all right. It could be managed. Put in its place. Eventually I even forgot the consultation, early in my marriage, with a doctor. I asked the doctor if I was frigid. He asked me what my relationship was to my father, and I told him that my father had died before I was born and that my mother never remarried. When I asked why he had wanted to know, he told me that sometimes frigidity is traceable to a persistent fear of the male, who continues to be regarded as a powerful and punitive father who is therefore potentially hurtful and damaging. As he spoke I realized that I had indeed grown up with a lot of suppressed anger that my father had died, leaving me without ever knowing a father. I asked the doctor if that could have something to do with it. He told me it was possible, but advised me not to push the situation as though it were a problem.

"You love each other," the doctor said. "Talk to Talbot about it."

But to do so would be inconceivable. It was too late. The lie was mid-sea, in full sail. And it worked. I was proud knowing I made order out of the chaos swirling around in that genius brain of his. His nervous system was such that to survive he was constantly on the alert, so that he wouldn't miss a new opportunity, and although his emotions were exceptionally strong he also had capacity for self-control, so that his passions were hardly ever displayed to outsiders. I sensed that early on he built up an adaptation of a "false self" compliant to the wishes of others, actually a mask concealing his true identity (except, of course, to me) and unlike most admired artists, who are disappointing to meet because their true identity is in their work and what they present to the world is either a false persona or else less than half of themselves, Talbot's chameleonlike charisma enabled him to adapt himself to any situation—like a great actor playing a part. No wonder people were drawn to him, and how I enjoyed the subtleties of his performances knowing it was only I whom he trusted, only I who had complete control, only I who had the aptitude to organize his life so that the irrelevant, the disorderly, the distasteful were eliminated as together we strived for perfection in meeting our inner standard of excellence. Together we were bright and beautiful, rich, envied, successful, structuring our lives as partners in all things, including our Talcilla. Why wish for more, I asked myself?

Now alone, during the day, scenes of my life with Talbot would appear superimposed over realities of my daily life, making it bearable. But by night others, clips of our lovemaking, inserted by an unknown hand, played like a movie in my mind's eye, came back until, wearied, I would block them out only to find they played on rewind again and again—a vampire sucking blood from the heart of our love. How exhausting it had been—the effort to contrive a performance every time we made love. With bitter regret I agonized, longing to confide in him, but the fear of losing him was so intense I remained silent. He might have understood—helped me work through the void. Guilt took hold as, lying in darkness, panicked, I clapped the right hand over the left, to find it ringless, having impulsively removed my wedding band and placed it on Talbot's finger as the lid of the coffin closed. A symbol of my going in the grave with him.

TALBOT ENTWINED OUR NAMES Talbot and Priscilla into the logos—Talcilla—and so our estate on the eastern shore of Maryland came to be known. It soon expanded into an architectural practice—the Talcilla Fellowship of Architects—farms, residences, drafting rooms for apprentices, and the annex to house Talbot's archives. It was at Talcilla that Talbot created his masterpieces and it represented in every detail the soul of our personal and working lives—our partnership. Of all our estates it was the one I loved most.

It was a heart-wrenching decision but the right one, after Talbot's death, to designate Talcilla a museum where present and future generations could visit the source of his architectural genius. Supervising the project consumed me, but what weighed heavily on me was that I kept putting off the day of opening the annex that housed his archives to curators—for once I did, it represented a final letting go. . . . And so I delayed. Until one summer night, as if sleepwalking, I rose, covered my nightgown with a robe, and, barefoot, ran from the house across the lawn to find myself leaning against the metal door of the annex, trembling. I opened the lock and stepped into that room I knew so well but had not entered since Talbot's death. Dazed, I gazed around at the built-in units sized to fit architectural drawings, files on another wall detailing in his hand the contents just as he had left them. I walked along the walls, touching labels, pausing at one marked "Private." Inside—letters piled one on top of the other, each neatly tied with string. Letters from parents, a sister, letters written in a hand hardly recognizable—mine, going back to my school years. He had saved everything. Pristine, in a neat pile, one on top of the other. I started opening at random, running my finger over the crisp white initials of my maiden name cresting the candy-pink stationery.

Dear Talbot,
Here I am after the divine Christmas vacation back at school, but all I think about is our meeting at the Metropolitan dance. My fat roommate

only thinks about food. All she wants to talk about are hot fudge sundaes.

All I want to talk about is you. Please write soon.

Love,

Priscilla

P.S. How do you like my new stationery?

Dear Talbot,

Why haven't I heard from you? Well, I'm busy too. Lots going on here. The Randolphs had a big party, friends coming from everywhere to celebrate the wedding. Lots of bubbly and many admirers (are you jealous?). Then Monday Ginny arrived so it's been one party after another.

We were in the Adirondacks last weekend and so you'll know what a serious person I really am, I'm sending a present I spotted in a store at

Tupper Lake. A burlap pillow with a spruce tree hand-painted in oil, inscribed "Spruce up and come—I balsam" (bawl some). Stuffed with real pine needles no less. I was going to say I painted this example of kitsch myself, but I'll never lie to you. So put your sweet head on it and dream of Pris. But why not take the hint—spruce up and come spend next weekend at the Ads? It'll be fun.

Love,
Pris

Darling Talbot,
Have you read Emerson's essay "Circles"? In it he says, "our life is an apprenticeship to the truth, that around every circle another can be drawn; that there is no end in nature, but every end is a beginning; that there is always another dawn

risen on mid-noon, and under every deep a lower deep opens." Oh, sweetheart, when I read this I think of us. How it's going to be when you place the wedding band on my finger, because our marriage will be a circle of truth that never ends.
Your adoring,
Pris

Under the pile of my letters I came upon another, tied with magenta grosgrain ribbon—dove-gray envelopes with writing in magenta ink in an unknown hand—Mr. Talbot Bingham, Box 964, Easton, Maryland. I turned an envelope over and saw the return address—Akeru, Montecito, California. From inside the envelope, lined with magenta tissue, I took out a sheet and studied a crest engraved at the top in magenta—a small but costly crown, and, under this, a bee.

I started reading . . .

Master,

One night, when you least expect it, when you are asleep and having only faintly uneasy dreams of an indefinite kind, I will appear in your room (because you once demanded as proof that you own me that I wear an invisible golden chain around my waist with the key to your apartment, I'll have no problem getting in the door). I will be carrying only a single match but that match will find its way to your body's middle, where, even as you sleep, you are thinking of me as I make my honey. It's as if that match is a bee that needs to suck your cock so much it could find it, hidden though it is, in the world's largest city.

And then, having lighted the way, the bee will fly away, the match extinguished, and I will begin, softly at first so that you can sleep a few more minutes, the long, slow, delicious process of licking your cock, and since I must have your honey-milk even more than the bee, I will struggle to stay quiet though my pussy will be throbbing drumlike; I will eat you at first around the rim of your cock in undulating circular patterns, until, as your breathing increases and your eyes flutter, I take it in my mouth and give it a special kiss. Master, I whisper as you surrender to our ecstasy.

B

Stunned, I collapsed onto the chair in front of Talbot's desk. Surely this must be some horrendous mistake? I looked at the envelope—yes, it was addressed to Talbot but the letter inside—no! There was no name save "Master." Somehow by fluke it had slipped in—but how? And who was "B"? The evil words a scorpion scrawling across the page—unable to breathe—more envelopes in the same handwriting—the magenta ink threatening, as if the words were written in blood. Shaking, I opened another . . .

Master,

I have just been taught a delicious game—something new. It will involve another, one you haven't met. Her name is Nadine. A recent arrival with a natural aristocratic air who more than meets our dear Maja's, big chief of Janus Club's, highest standards. Though petite, she resembles me, which is perhaps why Maja engaged her. Intrigued? Nadine's breasts, smaller than mine, may not be as much to your taste, but it will take only your glance for them to ·blossom into—peonies perhaps, palest blush, worthy of your special kiss. Yes, you are in for some-thing quite extraordinary—a pageant of sorts. Maja suggests I be present at one rehearsal so I will be more adept, no longer shy as I sometimes am when I participate with you, but I told her I preferred not to, as although I may have appeared reticent in the past, lately encouraged by your sensitivity I find myself more confident and hope it is not too forward of me to say that I feel competent to pres-ent myself in a manner that will please you. "As you wish," she answered, unconvinced, adding that Na-dine's charms will be formidable to contend with as she is far more experienced than I, but no matter— at least I may learn from her. Of course I am curi-ous as to what? Perhaps it will be a new delight I can interpret in my own way for your enchantment. Oh Master I long for this to be so, for my highest bliss is to give you pleasure. Now at last Maja's extending you an invitation—a week from today at Janus Club—precisely at nine for the Yab-Yum pageant. Don't be late. Maja, the ever-solicitous duenna of our establishment, will be present at the ritual to supervise her Byzantine taste for luxurious display. It will be a magnificent presentation—a fairylike scene of absolutely shameless imagination. Flowers are being flown in from Africa to be entwined in the glittering myriad prisms of our ballroom's pink crystal chandeliers; there shall be gamelan music and dancing dervishes. The benches in the first-floor gallery of the ballroom Maja is reupholstering in magenta velvet. The festivities planned are for you and you alone. You are to be the only guest participating in the Yab-Yum until toward the end of the ceremony, when, to add sugar and spice, Maja's worthiest members have been invited to join us for the Great Rite of the Yab-Yum, which promotes the belief that the sexes are equal in power, even that the female is perhaps the stronger, since no male entity could function without being united to her. At the ritual, all sacred coital postures in which a god or man is fully united with his goddess shall be explored. It will be a magnificent presentation—sumptuous kimonos from Japan, iridescent silks from Persia for cummerbunds to hold firmly in place the soft balsa wood of various shapes and sizes, not to mention sticks of gold tapered and beaten to silken smoothness—utilized only if the balsa is too malleable. There will be balls in a myriad of sizes, lacquered in coral, magenta, lemon yellow, purple, and acid green—filled with tiny bells. This morning Maja bade me pick papayas from her hothouse garden, scoop out the black seeds to dry in the sun. As I sliced the fruit in half I knew why she had asked me instead of Nadine to do this small task. She knows how susceptible I am to beauty, and the aesthetic of this image as I scooped out the seeds reminded me of a vulva, and I took delight anticipating that when dried they would be sealed in lacquered balls to become luscious toys to give you pleasure. Other implements of dazzling beauty will be on hand . . . of course this is only the beginning—pain of an exquisite kind comes later. But already I've revealed too much—for god's sake don't tell Maja about this letter—she'd kill me! She expects the Yab-Yum to be a surprise. But you have honored my ass by poetically calling it your "tulip," treating it with such respect and special favors that now it is time for me to be unselfish and let you do the same for another—Nadine. See I'm not jealous. I rejoice in the opportunity the Yab-Yum provides for the sharing of these pleasures. Maja teases us both, intimating it is to be a contest for you to decide

which to select for your "undivided attention"—and
"recipient of dreams beyond imagination." What is
all this about?
Bee

There was *no* mistake—these letters were
written to Talbot. Shocked, I started to read
the letter over, but there were more—and now
I knew her name—Bee. Dying, yet strangely
disturbed, excited—I opened another.

Master,
With mighty effort (I congratulate myself) was
I able to conduct myself with nerveless poise
throughout the Yab-Yum, despite the ravishing
beauty of Nadine who far outshone me I fear. But no
matter—for it is me you choose. That Maja made me

wait these many days before summoning me to her private quarters when after the ritual she knew your decision immediately is her way of asserting control of this establishment, but why not? It is after all her combination of wisdom, intelligence, and business acumen that makes Janus Club the oasis it is for I'm certain there is no club in the world where the members are treated so royally and with such courtesy and luxury. I knew full well she expected Nadine to be the one favored, but her ego is such that when informing me of your decision she intimated that she secretly had expected me to be the recipient of the honor about to be bestowed. "Yes, Bee," she said as I sat there not knowing what was to come, "when you first came to Janus Club I sensed in you a creativity that would serve us well—some creative people seem to have only a tenuous sense of their own identity, and I suspected that you came to us searching for yours. Talbot will give you opportunities to find it. You're like litmus paper, easily identifying yourself with others, but though multi-faceted as a diamond you lack belief in your own uniqueness, and therefore feel an especial need to assert yourself and preserve what you feel to be precarious—perfect qualifications for what I look for in my goddesses. But I cannot warn you strongly enough—you must hold fast onto the deepest part of yourself—this is the essential component of success—take a tip from Nadine, who is far more experienced than you, for she has mastered this well—so child, listen to your Mamacita—don't be foolish." I sat speechless as she congratulated me, going on to explain, "Talbot wants structure in his life and has set up a modus vivendi: The Rules." She cautioned in a motherly way how crucial it was to follow them to the letter if I was to make a success of my liaison with you and the good fortune it would bring. "Listen carefully, Bee. I know

Talbot well—he is incapable of real intimacy—the unconditional sharing of thoughts and feelings with another person so that they become almost another self—it threatens the complete inner freedom that is essential to him for his art. And like all artistic geniuses he suffers from mood disorders, bursts of energy, cocksure agility, quicksilver thinking, shadowed by streaks of irritability. He's _too_ generous, grandiose, takes too many reckless chances—his imagination is beyond grasp. If you can deal with all this you'll make a go of it—also accept that he alternates between orgies of work and orgies of pleasure—and in spite of his gross overwork he's almost always late in fulfilling contracts—but leave this territory to his wife, Priscilla, who from what I hear would be capable of managing IBM."

I begged her to tell me about her, but Maja shook her head. "The less you know about her the better it will be—don't think about her. She has nothing to *do with you." That will be easy for I think of nothing but you, over the moon that you have chosen me. I would have fainted dead away had I known that first night weeks ago when you first walked into Janus Club that your mission was to find a permanent Mistress—or "Maîtresse" as Maja would say. Had I known that was your intent how intimidated I would have been when Maja told me I was to sojourn on your yacht Talcilla (Nadine invited first). When she returned I questioned her, but she brushed me off, saying only, "They were charming days in the Caribbean." And a month later I found myself on the Talcilla, where time did not exist as we drifted in warm seas, swam in blue grottoes, had long leisurely lunches on the deck, prepared by your master chef Jean-Claude, of fish we had caught that morning, and after finding refuge from the heat of the sun in the cool of your stateroom, my body coming alive in ways I never knew existed, the surprises (finding the turquoise enamel Fabergé egg encrusted with sapphires—in an egg cup on my breakfast tray). Oh Master—more than heaven— paradise. Maja is puffed up with pride by success— not to mention that you have reimbursed her more than magnificently for my exclusive attentions and provided for Nadine who, although rejected, is also more than satisfied by your generosity, as are all who participated. After telling me my good fortune she handed me a small square cream-colored box, saying, "Talbot is in Switzerland as we speak but he left this for me to give you." I opened the box and nestled inside was what appeared to be a skein of silk rope, coiled like a golden snake, but upon being taken out of the box, it rippled down into a dress, pleats of softest silk stitched with gold-flecked Ve-netian glass beads. "This is a tea-gown designed by Mariano Fortuny," Maja told me—"one which* *belonged to Talbot's grandmother (well, reader, we know he's complicated)—these dresses are legendary, having been worn by the likes of Sarah Bernhardt and Isadora Duncan—described by Proust in <u>Remembrance of Things Past</u>. That he considers you worthy of wearing it tells us something about his regard for you." When I slipped it over my head it touched my body like the softness of a second skin slithering down into a pool of golden silk around my feet. Maja stood, admiring, telling me, "You'll wear this dress when you and Talbot are having tea—but on special occasions only. Choose them wisely."*

And then, oh Master, that day of days, that wondrous day when you came to claim me. Maja's atelier worked day and night to complete my dress— layers of white tulle embroidered with diamanté and crystal stars, the strapless décolleté fitting so snugly I could hardly breathe, or was it the ex-

citement of knowing that soon I would be forever yours?

The alcoves in the balconies around the ballroom were packed with astonished members of Janus Club as they leaned forward to witness my entrance seated on a unicorn (how in god's name did Maja find one? Only she could come up with something like this). Nadine and Rowena, veils of spangled gauze floating around the lush beauty of their bodies, naked save for jeweled thongs, Nadine's dark tresses entwined with pearls, Rowena's corn-silk hair sprinkled with jet and diamanté as they led the procession, beating tambourines on which floated silver and gold streamers interwoven with bells.

And there you stood in the magic circle, holding out your arms, as I leaped from the unicorn to stand by your side. Ceremoniously you opened a black lacquered coffer painted with fan-tailed doves and white blossoms, taking from it a ring—big as a lump of sugar, blue as my eyes, and placed it on the middle finger of my left hand, saying:

"Bee—this ring is a star sapphire called The Star of Destiny; it has three crossing rays favored on the gem signifying The Triple Goddess of Fate." From behind me someone (Maja?) was placing a mask fashioned from wings of a dove and marabou feathers over my eyes but all I heard was your voice saying:

"Akeru gods are supernatural lions guarding the gates of sunset and sunrise and between them runs the dark passage of the underworld through which the sun must pass each night. Akeru gods are two-faced Sphinx, a sort of animal Janus supporting between its heads the sun disc on the horizon. They are the lions of Yesterday and Today, their two-headed push-me-pull-you form is the symbol of Time and as I am taking you through a dark passage into light I have named our paradise Akeru and you shall be its Queen. It is deeded in your name with a fortune to support it and yourself forever."

Although my eyes were covered by a blindfold I swear I heard jaws drop as you revealed the generosity of this gift.

"Come Bee, it is time to set forth on our journey."

As you led me away to—I knew not where—snow sifted gently down on my face as you whispered, "Bee, my queen . . ."

The time traveled by plane was long and tedious, and I was sometimes fearful during the journey as you sat silent by my side not holding my hand or speaking.

At last we arrived. I could hear the sound of water which I thought came from a brook, but when you removed the mask I found myself standing by a fountain centered in the courtyard of a *house high in the mountains, overlooking valleys of green hills and, beyond, the sea. And lo and behold! I couldn't believe my eyes—there below us in the valley was the unicorn grazing on meadow flowers. Warm air caressed with the scent of night jasmine as the sky darkened, taking my hand you led me through a gate cascading with bougainvillea toward the house until we came to a double door crafted with mother-of-pearl inlaid in ebony. I stood marveling at the intricacy of a mosaic of a double-tailed siren inlaid in the wood, and, embossed above this—Akeru—*

"The double-tailed siren is the sea goddess, whose pose refers to the female mystery—see the crest I've designed for you—a crown and bee—there, between her double-tail."

Opening the doors you led me into the house through rooms splashed with color.

"Your colors, Bee, those which suit you best."

Emerald green, pale dove-gray, persimmon, the yellow of lemons, chartreuse, here and there pillows of magenta silk, and on mirrored tables, crystal bowls of apricot and mauve roses, pots of speckled gloxinias gathered from the gardens, porcelain bowls holding scented potpourri, until we came to our bed chamber.

Its simplicity startled compared to the extravagant rooms we had just passed through. Walls papered with silver tea paper, floors lacquered white as patent leather, and centered in the room—a bed canopied with gauzes floated by breezes coming through the white shuttered doors opening onto an enclosed garden, where a table had been set for supper, candles lit (by whose hand?). But instead of partaking of the repast, you made love to me for the first time in my own house, so tenderly, so violently, that I fell asleep unafraid in your arms (I'll remember that night forever).

At dawn I was awakened by the sounds of fan-tailed doves making love with tender monotonous cooings in the enclosed garden. But believe me Master, it was no fun as I reached out for you to find I was alone. Panicked I ran through the empty house, on out into the gardens where a woman dressed in black approached, her demeanor somber.

"Mr. Talbot had business to attend to and left early this morning. May I suggest shopping—there are fine shops near Montecito in Santa Barbara or a drive perhaps by the sea? The car is at your disposal."

It was that day I learned The Rule most difficult to accept. That your visits may be infrequent, and future visits will be decided by how I comport myself by expressing no signs of dissatisfaction or jealousy. Believe me, Master, you shall have no reason to doubt my behavior, which (sooner than you might think) will confirm I am deserving of—dare

I suggest?—more frequent visits. It matters not, for when you do arrive—such as at your last visit—you will be enchanted that I have filled a bowl with warm, sugared cream ready to circle my breasts, exciting them to swell into the size you most favor for biting. Knowing they were fair bursting to be treated less gently you held back until I couldn't stand it a moment longer and had to beg before you gave surcease with the mercy of your teeth. You never deny me. How can I not crave more? How can I not wonder how long must I be made to wait this time? You mentioned some trip with Wife, but when? And for how long?

Bee

My Beloved Talbot,
Do you know how happy you have made me? I thereby reiterate again and swear honestly and

truly to keep The Rules, confirm once again you own me exclusively, Master, to instruct in any manner of your choice. Also honestly and truly tell you— no man (or woman) has ever thrilled or excited me as you.

Royally you treat me and I am grateful to you with all my heart. No Queen has ever been given a more extravagant gift—a house designed and built for her by Talbot Bingham, described in <u>Architectural Digest</u> as "one who may be noted in history as controversial, yet perhaps America's most important architect." (I added this clipping to my Florentine gold-tooled scrapbook—a parting gift from Maja.) Not to mention the lavish presents of money put in trust, which gives me independence to never again have fears for the future.

Sometimes musing over days at Janus Club before we met, I must confess there is one girl there—a seductive, insinuating creature—Rowena, her erotic allure is such that she is quite as fascinating to many women as she is to men. I was drawn to her plumpness, which is that of a partridge; every time she settled into a cushion, as if nesting on unhatched eggs, I would fancy I was one, about to be hatched and find her sweet bottom to nuzzle into. We were all attracted to her (even the aloof Nadine), and, of course, she had a waiting list from members of Janus Club who paid dearly for her attentions. Though busy, she still took time off to give demonstrations. I was flattered when I was one chosen, for she is a magician with hand and tongue, never rough or hostile in her attitude, as some of the goddesses who secretly only prefer sex with men. Her manners never brusque or rude, always mindful of another's pleasure as well as her own. There never was a time I did not eagerly collaborate should she ask my assistance in stretching a new arrival's tulip, always taking into consideration the poor girl's fears if the client demanded it stretched too severely to better accommodate his cock. Instead, if the girl felt apprehensive, Rowena would suggest another, more experienced to deal with what can sometimes be an unnecessarily painful ritual.

It was Rowena who gave me—as farewell present the night I left Maja's—our collection of colored balls, connected by a string, instructing me to select the size to anticipate your mood of the moment, suggesting I pick fresh mint from our garden, warm oil slightly before bruising the leaves in it with mortar and pestle, adding a pinch of cayenne pepper, to release the fragrance. Dip the balls into this before giving me the pleasure of gently inserting them, one at a time, into your sweet bottom as my tongue circles your cock. The mint and cayenne gives a nippy tang you will enjoy. She cautioned not to let the string vanish up into you. But should that ever happen, there are intriguing ways of retriev-

ing, so never fear. When first we played this game you moaned, begging I be more aggressive as I pushed them up into you with my tongue, and oh! with what relish I complied. I hope you do not think less of me—now that you know in all fairness it was Rowena and not me who should be given credit for introducing us to this pleasure. I'm only thankful, Master, that you were never attracted to her and therefore it was your Queen Bee who first initiated this playful game instead of another.

Maybe I shouldn't be telling you this—might make you think I'm trying to make you jealous—but how could that be when you know I think about your cock all the time? And right now I am so keyed up it's all I can do to stop getting to my clit. But high on the list of The Rules you have strictly forbidden this minor diversion, even when I haven't seen you for weeks, and there would be a "small chastisement" should I disobey (although how you would find out is hard to fathom). Perhaps not, uncannily intuitive as you are.

Still I'm curious as to what it might be? I tremble. Deprivation of your cock necessitated by longer time than usual spent with Wife? Or, upon return, denial for an indefinite time of the bliss your mouth gives as it explores my body? Insistence I accompany you to Janus Club to select one of Maja's new favorites, even insist perhaps it be the dreaded Nadine (who I know you still fancy), for another sojourn with her on the Talcilla, this time to islands in Greece—a place you have never taken me—until satiated by leisurely discovery of her lovely body, you return, expecting me to be cheerful, exhibiting no sign of discontent?

No matter—I welcome any challenge. Nadine or any other would last fleetingly as the life of a butterfly at the paradise Akeru that you have given me. None have the love of beauty, the imagination, the fantasy to hold and nourish that combination of macho tenderness and feminine sensitivity I treasure in you. No. Not one. I'd bet my life on it.

And only your chosen one—me—has strength to accept that there is more, much more than a streak of cruelty in you despite your kindness and generosity, which is boundless. I experience it often. Surely you know it takes all my control to listen to tales of "Wife" and "Partner," when you point out photographs in newspapers or display pictures you carry in your wallet. I pretend not to care, because this perverse pleasure is included in The Rules (don't think it makes it easier to note that the house you built for me is far more magnificent than the one you built for her). Don't think it makes up for trips, disappearing to places you are secretive about, Greece in summer with Wife on the yacht Talcilla, named for your partnership; Aspen; the long trip to Bali discovering with her instead of me

*the magic of gamelan music, even though I suspect
your passion for music is a way of expressing emotion which is impersonal—it matters not, for each
time it is I who wait—my body swathed in invisible veils, a chastity belt, knowing the key to open
it dangles on your key chain while you are fucking
her instead of me.*

*I'm sorry, Talbot, to have brought this up. For-
get it, please. It breaks The Rules we have mutually
agreed on. But please, please—hurry home and for-
give my indiscretions.*

Exclusively yours now and forever,
Bee

Seething I read over—"don't think it
makes it easier to note that the house you
built for me is far more magnificent than
any you have built for her." Felled—struck by

a boxing glove, but instead of being KO'd, I opened another—

Master,

I broke a Rule. You'd discover it anyway and I'll never lie to you. Thinking of you and Wife in London staying away longer than you indicated was too much. But as I touched my clit, in my heart it was your hand instead of mine—a badge of merit you might grant me as you consider whatever chastisement is in store. Whatever it may be the release was worth it.

Dare I suggest to be placed fully dressed over our favorite ottoman (the one tufted with puffs of saffron-colored velvet), my bottom covered for a muffled first smacking warmup. That done, placed over your knees, skirt lifted, begging you to not restrain yourself in giving my flesh the seri-

ous whacking I deserve. An ebony smooth-backed hairbrush—most appropriate. The Mason-Pearson are considered finest, and it would be no trouble, while you are in London, to pick one up of a heft that pleases you at Harrods. You might take Wife to lunch at Claridges, and, after, she could go with you to select it. Her taste I hear is impeccable (see how angry I am). I am not suggesting this would be the light spanking occasionally administered by your hand with the reward of a luscious after-glow of warmed cocoa butter. No—a Mason-Pearson is a more serious matter. But no twigs, please. Too switchy and really painful. I had enough of that as a child from mean nuns at the orphanages, until I was old enough to have the wit and beauty which gave me power to run away.

When are you coming back? I'm getting itchy. Make it soon. I don't want to be chastised twice.
Bee

I tied the grosgrain ribbon from the letters around my neck and pulled. It crackled into my skin, choking me, as rocking back and forth I screamed at the cat who had wandered in from nowhere—what does it matter— what does it matter, as I ripped open another letter.

Heed, Master—

It did not sit well last night when you showed up with that—whatever her name was. She did have a pretty body, I'll give her that. And her mons mossy instead of waxed—don't think I didn't notice its scent came from her having been given access to the perfume you had blended exclusively for me on that last trip with Wife to Tangier, recalling how you elaborated on time spent supervising the mixing of frangipani, tuberose, and spices. Bet you had some cooked up for Wife too.

What happened last night isn't in The Rules. What new scenario is swirling around in that surreal brain of yours? Worst—she's a dead ringer for Wife—looks more like her than even I do—only not so skinny, thank god. How dare you bring her to Akeru without my consent. Don't think I didn't notice copper-burnished hair the shade of mine. I know Maja had nothing to do with this—friends there would have tipped me off. And don't think I've forgotten: when we first met it amused you to casually comment I was a type that appealed to you, because I eerily resembled Wife. That may have been a turn-on for you, but not me.

Let us go over The Rules. I am Queen Bee with full control over organizing your erotica, which gives your spirit freedom to pursue work so that your life runs smoothly. Was it only folderol you told Maja— that you'd found none qualified until you met me: "Bee has not only beauty, but smarts and though ap-

pears diffident with a gentle reticence—occasionally an unexpected take-charge attitude breaks through (absolutely!), which I find a charming combination not found in others I've been auditioning"—you'd taken "time to evaluate her character," coming to the conclusion "Bee is capable of keeping under control any tendencies of jealousy in her nature" (not necessarily), "carries herself with poise" you admired, suspecting "under her yielding demeanor there is a controlling streak in her nature (definitely) requisite not only for management of Akeru but structuring her own life by ability to respect and obey The Rules." And that "she also had intelligence and sensitivity capable of handling some tricky situation (which Maja didn't go into) concerning Wife." As you were still considering Nadine, Maja with her gift of sorcery consulted her oracle, concluding that position of planets at the moment when Nadine and I came together at Janus Club were significantly aligned, and, believing in the science based on the chaos theory postulated by Benoit Mandelbrot, showing how mathematically everything is literally and inextricably connected to everything else—a butterfly flapping its wings in the jungles of Brazil exerts an effect on the atmosphere here in our room right now—Maja knew the moment had come, there should be no more shilly-shalling, and she hastened to put in motion the Yab-Yum to discover once and for all which of us embodied all that you were seeking. Destiny brought it together and the outcome was—me. So that everything in your life "now fits easily, seamlessly into place," as you so often say. And so it has. Until now.

Stay away for a while. See how it sets. I'm not that crazy about you.

Bee

Pain ran up my arm as I beat my fist on the letter—how could he? "Everything in your life 'now fits easily, seamlessly into place.'" *I* gave him that. He told me so—praised me, acknowledged my expertise was what made him free to create without concerning himself with mundane details—the secretaries, household staff, apprentices, assistants—how painstakingly I interviewed and screened each and every one before I considered them worthy to be part of his entourage. How proud I was the day he named our estate Talcilla, cementing our partnership in every way. "High praise coming from you, my Lord and Master—thank you kind sir," I'd teased, giving a mock curtsey, and he'd bowed his head in deference, clapping his hands applauding. Oh god—what a fool I am. I started tearing the letter up—but instead opened another.

Talbot,

Having banished you from my sight until I cool off, I was caught off guard yesterday when you showed up at Akeru unexpectedly—so soon demanding punishment for past indiscretions. Lucky for you I chose the small whip weighted with tiny steel balls encased in cream-soft leather, dangling beguilingly from a handle that fits cozily into my palm, always a pleasure to wield instead of the cumbersome other (which you certainly merited). Keeping at it, I knew you wanted more, but the greater punishment would be to stop. So I did.

Your sweet fat bottom appeared more flushed and sore than usual, so instead of soothing unguents, I chose to finish it off with a few smacks from one of those newfangled kitchen gadgets you're always bringing home—which happened to be handy—some sort of thing with wire bristles— perfect to bring your cheeks to just the right shade of piggy-pink, ready for a sponge soaked in vinegar to rub on your bottom until you cried out in pain. Only then had you received punishment deserved. See how well I know you!

After this it gave satisfaction to demand compensation for my titties, which had been neglected for much too long. Your aggressive yet gentle teasing caused them to rise in ecstasy as you favored not one more than the other as you sometimes do. Both were given the attention I craved, plumped up until molto contento (as the Italians would say), fully satiated as your cock entered. By then I was wild with longing, unable to hold back a second longer (although I know how that pleases you).

Oh lover, it was divine. Fun too after, making that little supper of scrambled eggs, soft-cooked just the way you like, with a little beluga caviar folded in. The bottle of André Clouet 1911 champagne so icy-cold, so festive as we clicked glasses across the table and you humbly once again asked forgiveness.

All serene once more in paradise. But if you really want to get back in my good graces how about a little trip—a weekend in Amsterdam? The buzz at Maja's is that her charismatic nephew Pasha (remember he visited us at Akeru with his intriguing friend Volupia) has opened a cabaret there, which introduces diversions we might enjoy. Something not too bizarre but unusual, a surprise . . . surely you can come up with a reason—business, whatever—so Wife doesn't give you a hard time, complaining as she has lately that you're away far too often. I know it upsets you to see her in that mode. No doubt you will come up with something so she will let you go merrily on your way—what I don't care to think about.

X Bee

Drowning—gasping for air, panicked, the only thing keeping me afloat was to open another—

Talbot,

For the second time you have broken The Rules. Without consulting me, brought a girl to Akeru— again one with more than a startling resemblance to Wife.

As you introduced her—Dominique—I knew immediately why you brought her here without my permission. The minute I saw her I knew she was one I would never have considered suitable, bearing no resemblance to me—something about her— indiscreet and wild, with a reckless eye, which would only bring havoc into our paradise.

As you bid me disrobe her, I sensed you had encouraged her to take a superior attitude toward me, cavalierly ordering me to apply my milk-of-honey lotion to her body, your eyes on her with total disregard for me. Do you wonder why I left the room in tears, yet, unable to stay away, returned minutes later to find her spread out on the divan, eyes closed, your face buried in her pussy as she moaned in pleasure. As you continued I could feel my pussy creaming, knowing it would be she who'd find relief—not me. Unable to stop myself I touched my mons and as your delight in Dominique brought your efforts to fruition—my jealousy tearing me apart, as she came, so did I. But you, aware only of her pleasure, noticed not (at least I'll be spared punishment for this transgression of The Rules).

Rising from the divan, standing in front of the mirror, Dominique coolly appraised me. Maja once told me that the unbinding of a woman's hair by another may control cosmic powers and bring destruction, and although you might think this of no account it filled me with dread as I stood behind her watching as you leisurely unwound the braids around her head, freeing the copper-burnished hair, so similar to mine, touching it so tenderly as it rippled around her shoulders, moist from perspiration, and bid me comb it. "Hey—go easy there," she admonished when I pulled at the tangles. "Yes," you agreed, "don't be so rough, best get Rowena to come assist with the toilette." When I returned with Rowena I found Dominique searching among trinkets on my dressing table to find hairpins which she then poked into her hair as you were now rebraiding it, fiddling it into a crown on top of her head. "How charming," you enthused, bidding me go into our garden, gather morning glories, and upon return observe you playfully weave them into the crown. Anticipating your wishes, Rowena saturated a sponge with Eau Jasmine—handed it to you as I watched Dominique float in the scented water of the bath you had prepared as you caressed her breasts until her nipples rose into bud, worthy to be kissed. Oh Talbot, I hate you so.

I've never questioned The Rules. There was never any confusion. Maja had been fully briefed and so was I. You told Maja that you had come to a point where your "erotica had become chaotic, interfering with work and home," and passion for beauty inspired you to come up with a solution— Akeru—and so began your search for a Maîtresse worthy to reign. I will not let you take this away from me. I am your chosen one to be its Queen. I do, and have done everything to please you, followed The Rules to the letter. In the years ahead you may desire me less. This I am ready to face. And if that does happen, you will find me, as I am now, an eager collaborator whose only intent is to satisfy your most extreme wishes and fulfill your desires. Until I ran away from the orphanage—well, surely it is not difficult to figure out why control is important to me. I never had it—and now I do. It's my life, my happiness—it keeps me sane, balanced, gives me strength to explore my aptitude to perform as you would expect, to maintain Akeru a kingdom of beauty and pleasure unto itself for your delight in which I joyously share.

Maja knew full well what you were seeking and how to find it for you, the permanent Maîtresse, to stabilize your wandering attention span and restless spirit, a steward to be in full charge managing the erotica of your life. In return you would build Maîtresse a house (which you did—the paradise Akeru) to be in her name, putting money in trust for her independence and lifelong security. What woman who never had a home, loves sensuality and beauty, and cannot have children, wouldn't die to be blessed with this opportunity. I was bowled over and honored that you chose me. From the time I was born

I was in orphanages; never able to make a satisfying relationship with my actual parents, I stopped looking for this with real people—used my imagination to create substitutes for them in the form of idealized images. Who better than Maja to project onto her a fantasy image of nurturing Mother—and who more qualified than you, although you are far too young (age has nothing to do with it!), to project onto you the authority image of Father. Logically I know neither one of you will ever come up to what I'm seeking and that no matter where I look I'll always be disappointed. The only reality that is not a fantasy is Akeru and that belongs to me. And no matter how I hate you (sometimes), I still crave the power you have to turn my body into an instrument of joy as it pleasures your wildest fantasies. In love still with the image I've derived from my own inner world even though I know it bears little relation to the reality of you who receives it. I must have been mad, deluded, in thinking that you were the one person, the answer to life and all my emotional needs, but no matter: now aware of my errors, I'm determined still to continue following The Rules to the letter as Queen of Akeru, with approval of who enters our paradise. Be fair. Never again torment me with the sudden appearance of a Dominique, or the other, whose name I have mercifully forgotten. If bringing them to Akeru without consulting me was a test, you cannot fault me, for I passed it well. And remember it was you bid them leave, finally—not I. But let it be the last time you test me so cruelly. Never will you find one more capable of following and keeping The Rules than I—none more worthy to be Queen of Akeru.

I am so angry now I can say no more.

Your

Queen Bee who must be that—always.

Chips of pain rattled my head. Inside my body an octopus seemed to be growing, restless, its tentacles pushing me into altered states. Hallucinating, in a dream, Talbot was carrying me to a divan. Bee's voice, whispering bees on a summer's day—rain (but how so? as outside was blaze of noon) pattered on the roof—a sound so intimate lulling me into half-sleep, half-dream. Feverishly I sank into pillows as Bee's voice, soft, tender . . .

"Look Master, no doubt you didn't insist she wax her mons as you do mine—see—the silky hairs swirl beguilingly as on a cherub's head," and she buried her face between my legs—"there's a salty sweetness you might enjoy—her clit is rising slowly, but nicely—there, suck it, here—she'll like that. No—not

like that—this"—she grabbed his finger and pushed it up into her pussy, pleased that I suffered seeing that it aroused him—I felt myself open as a flower toward the sun as Bee took Talbot's hand, pushing his finger roughly up into me, causing me to cry out; dizziness overtook me as Bee's face came closer, merged into mine as we became one. I pushed her away and kneeled down, took Talbot's cock into my mouth as he stood, put his hands on either side of my head to steady it, whispering, "My darling, my love," thrusting his cock, faster and faster, up and down my throat, but instead of satisfying himself he pulled out and lifted me back onto the chair to face him, spread my legs, gently, not to frighten, kneeling down, explored with tongue and finger, lingering as long as I desired—my voice cried, "I love you, Master, I love you I love you . . ." melting into quicksand as his voice came from a great distance, "Sweet Priss, I know, I know."

WAS IT DAWN OR DUSK? Seizing the cat in my arms I hurried away from the annex, back across the lawn into the kitchen, and filled a bowl with cottage cheese. All left now was to eat it, wait half an hour—get something in my stomach, the article in the *New York Times* said—and who was I to quibble? Since Talbot died I'd thought about it often. Wait half an hour—then take the ninety Seconals I have collected. Five minutes was all it would take—and sure enough—I'd be gone.

How could I not have known that from the beginning he knew sex was distasteful to me—my joy, performance—lie, pretense, fraud. It wasn't enough. But why did he stay? Why not leave me? How like his genius to come up with a solution so as not to let the hassles our separation would involve affect his sacred art—a Maîtresse with the infuriating name of Bee to replace what I could not give him. But the letters? Are they left in the box among mine, stamped with an invisible tête-bêche for me to find as rebuke? Or a farewell message that in spite of it all, because he chose one who resembled me, I was his true love? No—probably it simply amused him to create a paradox that might (to some) define a possible truth. His dictum, like Goethe's, had been that the first and last task of genius is love of truth. But what truth? Was this Talbot's—that when sexual boundaries no longer exist it frees us to integrate our personalities into the boundaries the world expects, the demands it imposes? This filled me with terror, for it would be a place of untamed impulse, in which unspeakable fantasies, perverse desires, possessive love, and all other egocentric passions of infancy continue to exist unmodified by civilization or the process of growing up. And what of this Queen Bee in their castle high—Akeru—created by *her* Master—*my* Husband? What sort of woman could condone and be partner to this? Is she a chimera? A fire-breathing serpent, a snake with a lion's body, a second head of an antelope? If I could kill her monstrous guile, as in mythology, by pushing a lump of lead down her throat to be melted by her fiery breath, I would. How different their Akeru from our castle high—Talcilla—which Talbot and I created—did Talcilla exist only in my imagination? A ritual, a convention, a method of defense, a means of transmuting instinctive impulses to find expression in more appropriate ways—a standard method of control in which impulses and instinct are, as it were, tamed and allowed symbolic expression the world respects? Which castle is real? I torment myself—was it because Talbot possessed an unusual combination of qualities, rather than one particular attribute? Was the tension between these opposites and the need to resolve this tension the motivating force that drove him to create The Rules—Akeru—seek a queen for his realm? My beloved, bewitched into a Minotaur with the head of a bull living in the body of a man, devouring any person or thing as he lives in a paradise with this Bee person. It is she who is his Muse, <u>not</u> I, she who possesses his creative spirit, illuminating his body and mind with pleasures; as abandoned in a labyrinth of pain and misery I am torn asunder, the flesh of my heart they feed on. How can I not deny <u>She</u> is true Wife—not I. To her —no Minotaur—but beloved King Jupiter.

And Talcilla <u>not</u> the logos—Akeru. Oh the bitterness—the betrayal—with what objects had he surrounded her? Had he insisted on selecting the clothes, the jewels she wore, as he had with me? I must stop or I'll go mad.

PRISCILLA FELL INTO DEEP SLEEP, and when she woke she looked at the cache of pills, dazed to feel something like—hope? curiosity? dream/hallucination? Whatever it was had been awfully good—better than anything.

The cat jumped onto her lap and sat staring at her. She replaced the cap on the vial of pills. She got up to pour the cat some milk.

BY NEXT MORNING, reading and rereading the letters, I'd worked myself back into hysteria.

The letters became the only reality, and reality became dream as I put them in my suitcase and hurriedly left Easton for our house in New York.

My housekeeper Phoebe, after greeting me, retreated into silence, interested only in doing her job serving me my meals as requested, on a tray in the library in front of the fireplace, and making certain seasonal flowers were replenished in the rooms looking out over the river.

The bedroom I shared with Talbot had been lacquered and layered to simulate the shades of a seashell we'd found on a beach in Africa. A silvered screen painted with flamingoes he'd placed at an angle so the Balthus painting of a girl hanging over our bed, her legs stretched apart on a divan, a cat by her side, would be only partly visible on entering the room. I lay there under it, reliving the last time Talbot and I had been in New York, shortly before his death, to attend a charity function. I'd been on edge, as he'd been in one of his moods—distant, withdrawn on that brief trip, detached, until weeks later, on a business trip to Rio, in sudden desire on our way out the door, late to attend a business meeting, he pulled me back into our room at the hotel, closed the shutters against the blaze of noon and forced entry into me from behind, a form of lovemaking I detested but which I had come to adjust to, as, mercifully, he infrequently required it of me. But distasteful as it was, it once again restored me into an image of myself I could believe in.

THE POISON OF JEALOUSY consumes Priscilla as she acknowledges Bee to be Wife she was incapable of being. She brooded on the energy put into years creating a castle high that never existed. It was Bee who possessed the living, vibrant, passionate sexual side of the Talbot Priscilla had smugly believed belonged only to her. She could not deny it—Bee had won.

Now, IN NEW YORK, I would wake each morning and lie looking up at the chandelier, sun filtering through the windows, following rays as they hit prisms, my heart pounding. I placed a hand across my eyes straining to shuffle the shards of glass into a different kaleidoscope so as to divert me, postpone the torment awaiting me as I opened the drawer by my bed, knowing I would do nothing, see no one, but read and reread the letters, each time lashed into fury that Bee had known of my existence for years, while I had not known of her until the discovery of the letters.

ALTHOUGH ALWAYS DEVOTING an inordinate attention to her appearance, making herself look as seductive as possible for Talbot—Priscilla took brief respites from tormenting herself by looking in the mirrors lining the walls of her dressing room to reassess her body and the passion it had once provoked in Talbot.

Reflected back—a woman with copper-burnished hair swirling into patterns as if by mild breezes, which Talbot had loved running his hand through, watching as it settled back into a nimbus of light. Her complexion translucent, and, most unusual, the same texture as the skin of her body. Her eyes (although she wished for green) were the blue of true sapphire, set rather too wide apart in a triangular face of haunting delicacy, hinting at something off-beat—something you can't quite catch. A curious juxtaposition when devoid of makeup, her long eyelashes were jet black contrasting with the fairness of her hair, and without her having to fiddle with an eyelash curler or mascara they naturally swooped up into a sooty fringe accentuating those eyes. The nose, delicate, slightly retroussé. The lips suggesting a smile, and when it came it was as if a lightbulb had been turned on in a dark room. Priscilla dwelled on her broad shoulders curving down to the waist, imagining Talbot's hand circling, but she could not deny her breasts are those of a youth's, and as he cups them they are not hers; she imagines they are Bee's full ripeness, mocking herself as she thinks of Maja, agent who discovered Bee. She muses on another courtesan, Ninon de l'Enclos—hadn't it been she who said, "One needs a hundred times more esprit in order to love properly than to command armies"? Priscilla thought she'd had both—bitterly she speculates on why Maja knew instinctively what would appeal to Talbot, wondering if, in Maja's place, instead of Bee she would have promoted the plump Rowena or perhaps the shrewd Nadine? But she could not deny that the image reflected back appeared appealing— outwardly there was nothing cold or hard— only a yielding femininity that belied the coldness of her frigid heart.

My Darling Talbot,

I can hardly write as tears fall on the page. But of what use? You will never read this letter. Alone now as I was when premonition of death came, I write to anchor myself to you. I was in our bedroom reading and drinking my nightly ginger herbal tea when suddenly a ghostly presence made itself apparent emerging from the gate leading into our enclosed garden, approaching, covering the room in darkness. Something terrible had happened. Later when I told Rowena and others of this event, no one gave it credulity. But I know it was true.

The Rules—no more. This as it is the last letter I will ever write to you and so I am free to speak at last of my bitter jealousy of Priscilla, who has now once and for all claimed you. She—Wife to carry the flame of your genius. Wife to have the acclaim and respect of the world, Wife surrounded by loving friends to cosset and protect, Wife, the admiration of the life you and she forged together. Wife and the World do not know that I even exist. The Rules you now obey are hers: continuity of order, resolve, singleness of purpose bound into day-to-day truths of the so-called real world, while The Rules you chose for us were only a game and in death have no importance. Without support of the world by my side I grieve. What is left? For Maîtresse: Alone, supported by transient memory of a beloved that never was mine. For Wife: Husband, supported by power of the legend of Talcilla. How bitter these truths. I grieve alone without support of the world by my side. What is left? Memory and the beauty and luxury of Akeru. Maja always admonished us at Janus Club never to let the secret place in the center of our hearts be touched, for if we did it would be fatal. How bitter to learn that this is true. I let myself fall in love with you as Wife falls in love with Husband, not as your stony-hearted Priscilla but as a woman who is blessed with wonder of the heart. I'll tear up this letter after I finish it—although *what I'm really itching to do is send it on to Priscilla by overnight courier. It is imperative she read it. I crave she know of my existence. She must. She <u>will</u>. But in some strange way (I can't explain why) I won't. Perhaps because it would negate the memories of the paradise you and I created at Akeru, which is all I have left. In this realm you will always belong to me and I will always be your Queen. How could we have known this past week that your visit would be the last . . . .*

Hours in the enclosed garden by the marble fountain you'd commissioned in Florence, a scallop shell as one Botticelli chose for his Venus, and—on the ancient, ivy-covered wall above as on the carved doors to the entrance of Akeru—the double-tailed siren sculpted in my image, but with this difference: in my hand a cowrie shell with a gentle waterfall splashing onto the lilies below. Naked you'd carried me to the center of the fountain's shell, placing me precisely where the water, warmed by the sun, would trickle down between my legs finding the spot to please. Sitting back enjoying the effect it had on me, until concerned you'd hurried into the house, returning with a paper Japanese parasol to shield me from the sun as I called out, "Sing a song of Solomon— let my beloved come into her garden and eat his pleasant fruit." Laughing, you artfully entwined the parasol into the wisteria on the wall above the fountain, how relaxed you'd been, interested only in my pleasure as I lay back closing my eyes, but after a while wanting the pressure of the water falling between my legs to increase I reached out to you, asking your finger to follow the water as it trickled over my mons, down onto my clit, on behind my tulip before plopping into the marble scallop of the shell.

"No, sweet Bee," you'd smiled. "It amuses me to see if you can be aroused without my interference."

Enjoyable at first it became somewhat of a torment, drifting suspended in this slightly aroused state, longing for your finger to bring release.

You had no pity. I moved this way and that hoping to entice you as you called me sweet names—"my spouse of spouses, my milking honey bee, my cat of catkins"—as the nipples on my breasts puckered, swaying toward you I begged for your touch. Still you resisted—not even my mons, which at your bidding had been waxed, plumped up, as you liked, that very morning, patted with opaline powder to satin smoothness, tempted you. But nothing aroused me to your satisfaction—until you whispered—I could barely hear:

"Shall I insert you with a sweet carrot from our garden," and, as you said this, I overflowed in a stream of yellow salt-honey mixing with the sweet spring water dribbling down from the fountain.

"You've done well, Queen Bee, yes, well indeed,"

and, lifting me, you carried me back into the bed-
room and oh god, in an act of high spirits how joy-
ously we made love.
Good-bye my darling,
Bee

    Alone since Talbot's death Bee chose to
wear white caftans sewn by nuns in Florence
according to her specifications. Linen from
Rheims, others of gauze, raw silk, embroidered with magenta crest of crown and bee.
Silent, celibate as a Carmelite nun, angrily
she strides through house and gardens of
Akeru as a green poison runs through her
bloodstream distorting her beauty, turning
her into a creature screaming up at the sun
by day, "How will I live?" At night baying at
the moon, dream-traveling, she becomes an

eagle capable of controlling thunder, sweeping over valleys and hills, across ocean and mountains, waking at dawn to find her pillow drenched with tears as thoughts of Priscilla become a madness from which she must find surcease or die. She cannot accept that Priscilla has won—a plan starts weaving a web, but it's tenuous—it needs elaborating.

FROM DANK CAVES I shall summon demons to don their black hoods and at midnight when the fireflower blooms but once a year they shall be dispatched in rockets to capture Priscilla. Her screams crack the mountains as she attempts to escape, but she is blindfolded and stuffed into a box too confined even to accommodate her skinny body, only a small hole punched to let air in to keep her alive. Thus Mrs. Talbot Bingham shall be brought to Akeru.

Upon arrival, just about done in, she will be let out of the box, the blindfold removed. Welcoming her stands a giant figure of towering beauty, its face hidden by a mask of doves' wings and marabou feathers. Minions will lead Priscilla through gardens lush with narcissus, the scent intoxicating her into a state bordering on anesthetized. Ensconced she shall be in a cottage surrounded by tall pines under which lily of the valley and ferns, delicate as lace, sprout from patches of moss, moist with dew, where ominous mushrooms grow. She will be drawn into a damp, ferny dark by the beauty surrounding her in an unimagined world, tormented by the mystery as to what? Where? Why is she here?

Left with only a silent Rowena to attend

her, bringing her breakfast of bitter coffee, clotted cream, and lumps of dark sugar, croissants freshly baked and a particular jam, made, she will be told, of honeycomb mixed with black orchids from the giant figure's hothouse. She will question Rowena as to what is the flavor that makes her deliciously drowsy every time she partakes of the jam and who is the giant person? Rowena remains mum on both queries and after a time Priscilla wearies of questioning. Each morning after she finishes this repast Rowena removes the teacart and returns to the sunken tub of green malachite in the bathroom adjoining the bedroom to attend to her bath. As it fills, Rowena pours oils into the tub from a cruet which stands on a table with unguents and threatening objects Priscilla has not yet been able to identify. Rowena turns the hot-water faucet on full-force, so that it crashes down on the oil, releasing steam into the room with tantalizing scent that stirs Priscilla's memory, but of what? She starts to bathe herself, but with grace and poise Rowena will firmly seize the loofah sponge from her hand and submit her to Rowena's bathing not only her face but the intimate parts of her body, indicating when she should stand, bend over, before permitted to sink into the scented water. Actually it will be pleasant not to resist; Rowena's hands are skillful and more than once, between her legs, she will feel a sensation that makes her moan, bringing a nod of satisfaction from Rowena's usually impassive face. When the cleansing is to Rowena's standards, she bids her stand with hands above her head, but how unprepared she is, shocked by fistfuls of icicles Rowena hurls at her warm body to stimulate circulation. This is most unpleasant. She is bidden to step from the tub; she will be rewarded by the warmed terry robe Rowena wraps her into as she leads her back to her room where a brew of soothing belladonna herb tea sugared with meadowsweet honey-aphrodisiac awaits her. It will be pleasant to giddily loll back on the bed as Rowena, from a sumptuous array of kimonos hanging in a closet, selects the one she is to wear that day. Later she will be permitted to go into the garden and the day will begin as she meanders unattended down pathways leading into the forest among trees so tall that sunlight seldom glimmers.

At the edge of this dark forest Priscilla spots a Victorian pergola identical to one she and Talbot found on holiday in Cornwall. Yes—it *is* the very one but no longer pristine-white—it has been repainted a rich magenta. Garlands of honeysuckle trail from curlicued arabesques and saffron gauze curtains drift in the breeze ready to draw should privacy be indicated, and under the pergola cushions of magenta silk, left in disarray to lie around the centered dais. She stares, stunned as to how this pergola which Talbot had transported from Cornwall to their garden at Talcilla in Easton, Maryland, now finds itself here. Even more confusing is that although it is daylight, under the pergola it appears to be dark as night, as fireflies flicker in alternating patterns of stars and crescent moons intermingling with fairylike creatures; elusive and swift as hummingbirds, they dart from darkness into the sunlight toward her only to circle around her head and disappear back under the pergola.

Suddenly a group is seen approaching from a path in the dark forest. An astonishing sight: four figures wearing identical kimonos of lavender and saffron silk led by one of outrageous beauty—taller than the others—the giant person—carrying a banner emblazoned "Akeru," her robe a caftan of yellow gauze embroidered with crowns and bees. Over this, a cloak of magenta taffeta—its hood framing magnificent copper-burnished hair that wafts around her shoulders as she moves in stately manner toward the pergola. This image of frightening splendor is, of course, me. It will be the first time Priscilla has seen anyone save Rowena since arriving at Akeru, and, as our procession draws near, she will not know if we are friend or foe. But suddenly a reassuring huddle of black and white monkeys, led by my favored twin pets Oscar and Peter, scramble from trees in the forest, clutching in their tiny fingers castanets that they clickety-clack in improvisational rhythms, incessantly chattering in strange tongues as they hasten toward Priscilla in an overbearing but friendly fashion.

Rowena has been unobtrusively trailing Priscilla in her meanderings about the gardens and now it is time for her to spook Priscilla from behind a tree, pushing her toward the pergola, mumbling to sit on a cushion beneath it. As I take my place on the dais, Oscar and Peter separate from their *copains*, taking the banner from me to scurry up the pergola securing it on top, and come back down, compose themselves to sit and remain staring at her in a disconcerting manner. There ensues a silence, ominously threatening, as the sky darkens, but instead of rain about to pour down upon us, from the shadows of the forest an invisible group of skilled musicians start to play Talbot's favorite fifth movement of Beethoven's C Sharp Minor Quartet, op. 131. This has been chosen because it reminds me of Talbot's pattern of lovemaking: expectations first denied; then fulfillment, progressively postponed by fragmentation of rhythm, but at the very moment when rhythm, harmony, texture seem all but destroyed, the little fugue that opens the movement raises hopes and redirects expectations and returns to give fulfillment. Is Priscilla sensitive enough to pick up on this? Apparently not, for she is far too interested in getting a look at goddesses Galaxy, Volupia, Milo, and Luna, seated serenely on cushions well aware that as long as they are beautiful they

are alive. "Pay attention Miss Priss," I repri-
mand the cringing Priscilla. "There is to be
a three-minute silence in which you must
squeeze your eyes so that your face becomes
a tight little fist as it strains to think positive
thoughts to prepare yourself." But for what is
not revealed. "If you open your eyes even for
a peek there will be serious consequences."
Priscilla scrunches her eyes tight, her face be-
coming an unfortunate ball of hysteria. This
pleases me. I give release by tapping her bent
head—time to wake up. Finally she dares look
at me—stunned by the startling resemblance
we bear to each other. I return her glance
with icy stare advising she turn her attention
to the others present instead of ogling me, for
they have often enjoyed intimacy with someone she knows well. I let her take a good look

and order her to select one, assist her onto the dais, and remove her kimono. So as not to displease me she quickly complies. It is Milo she has chosen, and, as Priscilla removes her kimono, bathed in the dappled light filtering through the leaves of honeysuckle garlanding the pergola, the naked Milo stands a wonder of nature to behold.

"You have selected wisely, Priscilla, for Milo is one Talbot has enjoyed for special intimacies the others have never been able to get the hang of. But Luna, Volupia, and Galaxy each will have their turn on the dais when you will have opportunity to comment in detail which in your opinion Talbot has most enjoyed fucking. If you select correctly you will spend time being instructed in things I don't have time to go into right now.

If the goddess you select to be your teacher gives you an A-plus I shall deem you worthy to observe a video of Talbot fucking me and then you'll really learn a thing or two. If not— god help you."

On a whim I suddenly feel sorry for the poor girl and suggest her hands be bound with silken cords while Rowena pushes her down into a mossy bank where lily of the valley grows. But she resists and I have to resort to nodding to Rowena and Milo to part her legs to restrain them so I can readily avail myself of her clit, which I do with such expertise she comes instantly. It amuses me and the others that I am able to make her come so fast.

This was a good one! I am somewhat mollified, but only temporarily—it needs elaboration . . .

ALL MY ENERGIES are put toward organizing a fête champêtre in honor of Priscilla. Invitations engraved with my crest are speedily dispatched to friends of Janus Club as well as WASPy friends of Priscilla and Talbot from the eastern shore of Maryland and elsewhere. None decline.

Maja accommodates by hastily making costumes from sketches I have sent, which the atelier is to fit on eight of Maja's finest goddesses who are to be contestants at the gathering. Actually the costumes are but extravagant petticoats—layers and layers of silvered gauze placed between tissue-thin taffeta in rainbow colors, imported from Milan, made extra full. Talbot likes them so, for as he says full skirts beckon to "heaven underneath." I shall personally scrutinize attention to the tops of these costumes, fashioned from glittering stars gathered from the galaxy to sprinkle onto pink clouds that I spirit down at sunset and drape around the naked torso of each goddess. But before this the body is prepared by coarse sea salt, bringing skin to glow before application of scented gardenia oil. This is absorbed instantly, leaving the skin receptive to application of my own peach-tinted basecoat, blended with a smidgen of my meadowsweet honey-aphrodisiac, so when applied to torso I can let loose shaking onto the breasts a goodly amount of chocolate sprinkles, which will adhere prettily. After this my collection of huge goose-down powder puffs shall be brought forth and dipped in bowls of glittering silver and gold powders to generously pit-pat over the torso and face to complete the package (so to speak).

The luncheon will be preceded by entertainment on the terraces overlooking the sea. The day will be perfect—hot but not too hot—cool but not too cool. Peacocks fanning their feathered tails into plumes of iridescent splendor will wander with the guests among the gardens and pavilions. There will be strolling guitar players, champagne, laughter as a team of monkeys frolics among flower beds of hibiscus, petunia, gloxinia, and other speckled, mottled, and dappled flowers too exotic to go into right now, and, for eccentricities more or less amusing, Oscar and Peter singled out and brought forth to acquit themselves somewhat inadequately on the harp before performing their voluptuous extravagant tricks with their saucy *copains*, heralding a sumptuous buffet is in the offing.

Talbot's master chef Jean-Claude has outdone himself coming up with a menu that leaves even guests accustomed to unheard-of luxury goggle-eyed. Black risotto, potted lobster, lamb's ears with sorrel, hare croquettes, cutlets of wild boar, turbot with champagne, and suckling pig with eels. After guests have stuffed themselves with these delicacies they will further stuff themselves with desserts of fritters of elderflower, pistachio cream, and so on until by now fully satiated Talbot seated opposite me will catch my eye, stand, bow to Priscilla on his right, and extend his arm to her. She appears confused, but rises, and together they lead (leaving me behind, a shepherd to herd the flock) on into the forest to a secret grove of birch trees, where we settle down on cushions spread on the grass among wicker hampers which, when opened, reveal more rich food—candied kumquats in honey-dew syrup, babas drenched in rum, islands of puffy egg-whites floating in yellow custard cream, profiteroles in warm dark chocolate, pink cotton candy in lace cornucopias. There, in a merry mood, couples loll on the cushions in languid sensuality, sipping Château d'Yquem as the pièce de résistance—white peaches embedded in Parma violets—are passed in wicker baskets to the guests by minions dressed in Pilgrim outfits (an amusing touch to make Priscilla and Talbot's WASPy friends feel at home). *Marrons glacés* come next, served with liqueurs, but suddenly Talbot breaks the mood. Clapping for silence he points to a rock which glitters in the sun as if embedded with diamonds—an illusion, of course, for it is but isinglass—no matter—

"It is time for th / *divertissement*! Each to have a turn against the magic rock."

Now it is my turn with the energy delight brings, to circulate among the guests as I present each gentleman with an object (no illusion, believe me) while Talbot continues:

"As you see, my Queen is graciously presenting each with a golden clamp engraved with crest of crown and bee, and with it pots of unguent I brought—quite precious, discovered by chance at a somewhat bizarre ceremony in a monastery in a remote region of the Himalayas; a most curious aphrodisiac. Only a smidgen necessary—results work pronto no matter where applied—the recipient will be itching to receive your cock. But today this pleasure is to be denied. The game is to excite breasts only in any manner you fancy until you deem them aroused enough to receive the golden clamp.

"Come, sweet Pris, honored guest—you shall be the first contestant."

Talbot goes to where the agitated Priscilla languishes on the grass and brushing the aphrodisiac on his lips, leans toward her. As he does, her nipples pop up into *fraises des bois* so tempting he bends down and kisses one, then the other, far longer than necessary.

I am about to stop this nonsense, but sensing my interference Talbot gets in a quick lick of the chocolate sprinkles off her breasts, before hastily pulling her up and escorting her to the enchanted rock.

"Be brave, my Pris." He stands back, beckoning to me.

"Come Queen Bee." He hands me the pot

of aphrodisiac, and, clearly more interested in Pris than in me, instructs me I am to do the anointing, adding distractedly, "One only—only the left—the right is to be left untouched."

Priscilla shivers, her right breast shrinking as the left one rises to delicious ripeness causing Talbot to comment on it.

"Both—please Talbot," Priscilla pleads. "Rowena says it will hurt less if both are clamped . . . I beg you Master."

"Ah yes, but not today, Pris." Talbot is firm. "Come now, no tears—"

To alleviate her distress (always at the ready) I pull those goose-down puffs out of pockets in my skirt to fluff across her breasts for surcease but instead they find their way into an ice bucket and out they come—soggy mops of icy water which I impulsively let loose dippy-dabbing them erratically across her breasts as she shivers, trembling—"Oooo, oooo— Oooooo."

"That was quite unnecessary," Talbot says sternly. "Enough—now—we must proceed. As you will discover, the game requires patient teasing to arouse, which I shall demonstrate with Pris until she is ready to receive the golden clamp. And when so—after the first tweak of the screw—I shall use my judgment by moments of respite between tweaks. Do not be deterred by pleas for mercy, which may excite you to lose control—the art is in gradual tightening. How capable she is in participating in this game will reveal the hidden nature of her sensuality. Does she find pleasure? Or distaste? Is she the Maîtresse of your dreams or must you seek elsewhere?"

With that Talbot takes the golden clamp and deftly clickety-clicks it onto Priscilla's left breast and as he does this she cries out.

Rowena and the others wince—soon it will be their turn and they vow not to display emotion as Priscilla has.

But I am not pleased with Talbot. He is far too hesitant; moved by Priscilla's tears, instead of tweaking further he kisses her face, mumbling some mumbo-jumbo so low I can't hear a damn thing. Then he has the effrontery to cup his hand around her other breast, pitty-patting it tenderly.

"Enough!" I call out, pushing his hand away to give the screw a hefty twist myself. Guests cry out in protest as Priscilla faints. I solicitously fan her with a napkin and douse her face with a good dollop of sticky Strega liqueur as Talbot hastily removes the clamp revealing that under her nipple a small bee has appeared.

This image imprinted on her flesh somewhat soothes my boiling temper and I look questioningly at Talbot.

"Doesn't this signify," he says, relieved, "that Wife is slave to Mistress? Don't you all agree?" he asks the crowd, as emboldened by rich food and spirits they applaud and yes— some even whistle uncouthly. "But, all things considered, Wife has acquitted herself well, and is she not worthy to be fucked by me this very night?"

"Yes! Yes!" I sing out, quite giddy by this turn of events, "and let it be in the bed we share—what better place to show off her icy, icy, cold as ice, frigid heart."

However, later I reconsider. This has been a mistake—she will not be fucked by

Talbot—in fact she will not be fucked by anyone that night, but sent to bed in a cot in a dark room no bigger than a closet without any porridge or even a bite of supper.

Next morning, sitting in intimate dishabille over hot chocolate with Rowena we gossip about the events of yesterday.

"Umm—it was interesting . . ." Rowena lapses into silence.

"What—*what* was interesting?"

"Pris—did very well considering—"

"Considering what?"

"Well, in my opinion, Talbot should have clamped both breasts instead of only one—none of the others who participated were treated so—"

"I don't agree at all! He should have twisted the golden clamp *far* more aggressively."

"I don't know what makes you so mean—you never used to be like this—vengeful."

"What victory—my bee imprinted on her flesh. But it will fade. Next time I shall tattoo it myself, personally."

"Maja did indeed do a splendid job in choosing her finest goddesses to send from Janus Club—although it was a bit much for some, except for one canny beauty—what was her name? Who with remarkable grace withstood her partner's ardor with the golden clamp, seeming even to enjoy, without pretense, the delicious pain. She'll go far, that one. But I still say Talbot should have made it easier for Pris—after all she is Wife."

I give Rowena a slap. "It was Talbot's choice to clamp only one of Priscilla's breasts."

"It was Phoebe—yes, now I remember—Phoebe."

"Shut up, you idiot—who cares what her name is!"

"Calm down, calm down, Bee."

"Oh Rowena, I did enjoy myself."

BEE WAKES WITH NO MEMORY of these events save for the nagging fury of having a dream she can't recall. The weeks pass, but the more she attempts to remember the dream, the more it eludes her.

IN NEW YORK I grow increasingly restless and although our house is furnished and decorated to perfection I start changing it. Carpet suppliers, upholsterers, and painters are summoned, but when it comes down to it, I dismiss them, leaving everything as it was although it no longer pleases me. Instead restlessness fuels extravagance and I go to Fred Leighton's, where I purchase a Georgian Maltese cross pendant encrusted with rose diamonds. The spiritual comfort it brings suits my mood perfectly, and, spurred by success of my purchase, I hasten on to Cartier where I spot a ring, a hunk of sapphire blue as my eyes—"A star sapphire known as the 'Star of Destiny,'" the vendeuse confides, "it suits you well, madame,"—and what's more it fits my middle finger to perfection, but once home, flashing it in front of the mirror, I am dismayed because I can't find the three crossing rays favoring the triple goddess of fate that shone so brightly when placed on my finger at the jeweler. No matter—it no longer captures my fancy. Nothing distracts me. I long for sleep, for only then do devious plans going round and round in my brain free themselves by fruition into dreams at night, which momentarily assuage my angry heart.

I *must* see how she looks. But am I ready? Am I beautiful enough? Thin enough? Gaining as I have a few pounds since this happened, stuffing my face with the damn Teuscher chocolate truffles I can't seem to get enough of. A few days at the spa at Canyon Ranch will give me courage. Yes—and then my jet will speed me to Santa Barbara, my Rolls-Royce will meet me at the airport, drive me to Montecito—on up to the top of the mountain to Akeru. Hearing a car approaching Bee will run into the courtyard to see who it is—at last I shall come face to face with her.

As my chauffeur opens the door and Bee sees who is stepping out she turns ashen and faints dead away onto the cobblestones. Rowena, followed by her minions, who have been peering out the window, rush forward and carry her back into the house.

Following behind I leave them uselessly fluttering around the dolly-mop Bee has become as they attempt to revive her. From the looks of her she'll be out of it for god knows how long, giving me time to roam through the house unchaperoned. It is as I expected— the house, the rooms—everything—more magnificent than any house Talbot has built for me. There is reason to be jealous. Here— an aura of comfort, cozy opulence, seductive and beguiling, which I was never able to convey in the ambience of the houses Talbot and I lived in. Why is that? But now I must pay heed only to myself. It has been a shock to come face to face with Bee. We *are* eerily alike. I doubt if friends could tell one from the other. Even Rowena and her minions despite their concern for Bee are stunned, I could tell, by the resemblance.

Finally, coming upon Bee's bedroom, I stand looking around, mesmerized . . . so this is where all that fucking takes place. Looking out through a window I see a spot of white moving far below—an animal of some sort grazing in the valley. It starts moving and as it bounds away I perceive it to be . . . a unicorn! Good god—this slap gets to me more than anything thus far and I express my rage by messing up her bureau drawers, randomly fishing around, and, although I myself have dresses, linens, and garments exquisite as hers, I can't stop from lusting over charmeuse nightgowns trimmed with Valenciennes lace, silken thongs, handkerchiefs, brassieres (too large for my tiny breasts), livid to see not only embroidered on them, but embossed on everything, everywhere I look—the bee, the small but costly crown that drives me to madness. It's even on her goddamned gold toothbrush. Now that I am at last in her bedroom I allow myself to lie down for a rest on the bed where she and Talbot enjoy their fearful pleasures. Lying there considering my next move I have to admit I am hard put to come up with anything even remotely adequate to top the theatricality, the pandemonium my arrival has created. The whole scene has gone perfect to plan, but jealousy is exhausting me and I seethe with emotion imagining Talbot lying exactly where I am now, fucking her and not me. What can I do to quell raging fires?

It might be effective to dress in one of her gowns and find my way back to the living room where I left her—prostrate, passed out—to flaunt my beauty which is at its peak right now after days at the spa. Yes—that notion gives me energy to open a closet, but it is filled with white caftans too celibate for my mood. In others I recognize dresses of emerald-green, apricot, saffron, cinnamon— in styles and colors Talbot chose for me. There is not a dress in this closet that would not suit me to a tee, but I settle for a magenta chiffon and, taking off my dress, slip it over my head. When I stand to see how it looks in the mirror—I see it is not me but Bee, fully recovered, standing in the doorway. But is it really? We look so alike, might it only be a reflection of myself in a mirror? Ideas like pellets of quicksilver pound my brain into migraine as I try to free one into action, but they only make me crazy.

Next morning I wake, fully remembering each delicious moment. What a sublime dream! I write it down instantly so as not to forget it. This one *must* be at hand, to read again and again.

I CAN'T STAND IT a moment longer. I have to see where Priscilla lives. A foray to New York is put in motion, although somewhat delayed by indecision as to what to wear. Hours are spent trying on one dress after another as Rowena sits silent except for nods of approval—yes, or shakes of head—no. I am hard put to decide, as there is not one dress or suit in my wardrobe not selected by Talbot, each in perfect taste but sexy. Definitely. Rowena finally loses patience, and, sensing I am losing my audience of one, I hastily throw whatever is at hand into my suitcase and off I jet to New York to be met by limousine and chauffeured to Sutton Place.

I ring the doorbell and am shown into the living room by Phoebe, Priscilla's housekeeper, startled by her astonishing eyes, opalescent as green grapes, which look me over as she pleasantly tells me, "Mrs. Bingham has been expecting you." It's a long wait as I sit on a sofa until finally I hear heels clickety-click down the staircase. Suddenly there she is—in person—the hated Priscilla—who sits herself down on an identical sofa opposite me. It is

as if I sit on a sofa looking at myself in a mirror. We are both dressed in identical jackets
of chartreuse jersey wool, navy skirts, navy
hose, and spiky-heeled shoes. We even have
the same-patterned Hermès scarf artfully
placed around our necks. Priscilla asks if I
would like tea.

"What I'd really like is to see the house."

"Of course—come!"

Priscilla graciously minces up the stairs
curving to a long hall. Unable to contain myself I say,

"The bedroom first if you don't mind."

"Of course—that's where we're headed—I
knew you'd be interested—"

She leads me into a room looking out
over the East River. The first thing I spot
is the chair. It is exactly like one in our

private sitting room at Akeru, one that Talbot designed, covered in a cinnamon fabric with a pattern of magenta squares, ample, wide, with rounded padded arms, the upholstery soft as marshmallows. A chair I love to sink into, reading, and often Talbot had tried to distract me, taking the book from me, lifting my skirt, skimming over my mons, continuing until it honey-creamed to his satisfaction, then kneeling down, spreading my legs, and, with great deliberation, circling my clit with his finger, and as it rose I begged for more, knowing in time he would touch it with his tongue—and oh god—what better way of whiling away an afternoon.

Priscilla sees me looking at the chair and comments, "Talbot designed that chair, the fabric too—I often sit there reading."

I went over to the window and looked down at the river as the tugboat *Tom Tracy* chug-chugged by, projecting myself onto it, imagining I was there and not here.

"We love this house," Priscilla said coming over to stand beside me. "Such a contrast from our other homes—the farm in Maryland, the flat in London, the pied-à-terre in Paris, the cottage in Nantucket with its heavenly sea and blue sky."

"You know what I'd really like now is not tea but a glass of sherry."

"Of course, we'll have it in the library." I follow her and once again we sit facing each other as Phoebe, eyes averted, silently brings a cut-glass decanter of sherry and glasses on a silver tray, placing it on the coffee table between us.

My hand shakes as I reach to take the

glass Priscilla is about to extend. Instead I open my purse and take out an envelope, handing it to her.

"What's *this*?" she asks.

"A letter—"

"Of what interest to me?" she says dismissively.

I remain silent.

"Why it's *Talbot's* writing."

"You're welcome to read it."

I put out my hand to take the letter back and stand up, but she's got a real grip on it.

"I have to go. If you want to read it, it will have to be now."

She takes the letter out of the envelope—

"Out loud," I say.

The two of us sit for what seems like hours, but perhaps it's only a blink . . . trembling, she begins . . .

My Dove, Sweet Bee,

An envelope will be delivered to you by a stranger and inside will be a ticket for a magic show. It comes as a great relief as you have waited so long, scented and coiffed exactly as I wish, your hair braided loosely and held by tortoiseshell combs, tendrils falling gently as antennas of mythical creatures around the pale beauty of your face, lightly tinted by a maquillage that allows its luminosity to shine through—and the sapphire blue eye shadow flecked with silver, please—your mouth made ready for kissing by a sweep of candy salve. I mentioned to Rowena to pull the laces on the bodice I brought from Neverneverland extra tight so that your breasts will poof up deliciously, longing to be released to my tender mercies—and, of course, you are wearing my preferred leather emerald-studded collar, but as I your Master have the chain and haven't come, the strain of waiting in vain for me so many nights makes you question your mental integrity. The magic show will be a most welcome diversion and one you richly deserve. Nevertheless you must leave notes for me everywhere explaining where you are just in case I come for you.

Though the magician performing at the magic show may be rather pedestrian—producing the usual rabbits and nosegays out of ostensibly thin air—you will, I guarantee, enjoy yourself immensely, in spite of the collar you are wearing, which is itching, even irritating, your neck. On balance, your mood will be good and you will smile and be eager to cooperate when the magician picks you from the audience to help him perform his trick. I have ordered him to whisper to you on stage, "Don't worry, I know what I'm doing," and don't be put off by the heavy white makeup he is wearing, which might *make you apprehensive; once it's removed, he can be trusted. As you enter the casket he will mutter, "Cooey-gooey conga" and a lot of other gibberish as you feel the casket spin like a wheel until suddenly you will find yourself deposited back on the stage, but no one is applauding, because you are clearly in another place than the one you were in before you entered the casket, and, as you look out into the audience, you find it too to be not as it was before. You may be surprised to find standing beside you not the magician—but me. You will long to ask how I made everything happen, including the new audience—what my connection is to this magic show, do I know that it is me myself? But you will remain silent because you want to have your pussy licked so badly you think you are about to faint with longing, and don't want to risk irritating me with idle questions.*

"Heel," you'll hear a voice say, overjoyed to discover it is mine; you will happily get on your hands and knees as I tell you, "Now do what you're supposed to do"—turning my back I'll bend forward over a chair, rest my arms on the seat cushion, as your hand slaps my bottom until spots of pink appear, which you'll lick and soothe until the heaven of your face finds its way tight up against my tulip, your tongue at last doing what it is supposed to do, seeking deeper up inside me.

Nadine will appear from nowhere to reward you with a special treat, circling your nipples with her finger, expanding pleasure by taking a breast into the lovely wideness of her mouth while squeezing the nipple of the other with her fingers into a tiny bud of pain as your pussy honey creams with anticipation.

But suddenly we will be interrupted by

Maja, of all people. How like her not to miss an opportunity to appear center-stage when festivities are about to peak. Startlingly dressed in a vermillion robe and cape similar to that of a cardinal or archbishop, twirling jeweled fingers in arabesques around her head, she will produce a galaxy of bursting stars, from which a naked girl will appear. The audience, clearly delighted, will applaud. At once I will notice the chain circling her waist is the very one I had made for you in Florence by Bucellati, a chain of such delicacy it is invisible, on which hangs the golden key bearing my name. How the hell did she get it? Certainly not from you? The girl will diffidently stand back as Maja brings her forward to introduce her as Phoebe. I observe a somewhat awkward maiden with eyes, feline, opalescent as green grapes and such exquisite features no *wonder Maja considers her a prize. Her hair, a startling shade of amber, cascades, a waterfall of silk, down her back as I remove the invisible chain and attach it onto the leather collar around her neck, which for some reason displeases you. Phoebe's mons has enormous appeal as Maja has wisely left it unshaven and it presents itself a tuft of amber softness. How thoughtful of Maja to imprint your crest of bee and crown placed on her flesh, precisely at top of the V where the mossy tuft begins.*

Here Priscilla is unable to continue. . . .

"I've had enough of this," Priscilla shouts.

"As you wish." I stand reaching for the letter, ready to leave.

Abruptly she changes her mind, sits down. . . . starts. . . .

But never fear my Queen—Phoebe will be but a passing fancy—but come, come now—no more sentimentalities. I ease Phoebe into the chair, contemplate her beauty, as tentatively she leans forward to take my cock into her mouth.

"No, no, that will never do," I interrupt. "I can't hear you—speak up."

She wants to kill me . . . but instead a coughing fit ensues.

Opening my purse, urging her to calm down, I offer a soothing lozenge readily at hand, leaning across to pat her knee, saying, "There, there, dear."

"Shut up," she says, rudely brushing away my hand, but mesmerized by curiosity delves back into the letter and proceeds in an acceptable manner.

"Louder," I say.

As I stand thus, jealous of her interest in me you kneel, exploring my balls with your glorious tongue. You know I prefer giving prolonged pleasure before possession, but your expertise excites me and, unable to restrain myself, I thrust my cock, aggressively moving back and forth, into Phoebe without further ado. This makes it difficult for you to keep your tongue in place, and, as the audience finally becomes aware of the degree of difficulty, they do in fact applaud for you. But does this please you? Instead you begin to cry, your tears lubricating the outer rim of my tu-

lip, and, always solicitous of you, dear Bee, not wishing to distress you further, I extricate myself from Phoebe, ensconce you in her place, spread your legs over the arms of the chair, swallowing the hot honey (even hotter than your tears) that is streaming from your pussy. How delightfully receptive you are. When finally you can hold back no longer, beginning to scream, your orgasm begins, the audience, now completely on your side, erupts in applause, and, as they do, Nadine, Phoebe, and Maja vanish, leaving you, Queen Bee, triumphant to find the invisible chain with golden key dangling once more around your waist.

Are your fears at rest? I hope so. I am perhaps overly sensitive to your moods, for lately you've exhibited signs of a jealousy which surprise me. Put my mind at rest, please, invite Phoebe to join us at Akeru for an indefinite stay as I shall be coming there next week. By complying you will prove how misguided I have been in misinterpreting your actions perhaps intended as provocative preludes to our revels? Phoebe deserves to be educated in the art of enjoyment, for I suspect that she, like my wife, Priscilla, is sadly lacking in the ability to accept pleasure, which accounts no doubt for her lack of expertise at the magic show. It sometimes crosses my mind to ask you to invite Priscilla to visit Akeru so that you could administer to her the same attentions I expect you to extend to Phoebe. How I would welcome any change this would make in her and how I would cherish you, dear Bee, even more than I do now for even a small transformation you might enable her to achieve so that she could in some measure experience the pleasures we enjoy. But I digress— Phoebe is another matter . . . she's an interesting girl. I suspect she moves on strange planes as you do, Bee, and perhaps blessed with your chameleon skills of transformation? But needs encouragement, as you once did, to become confident, trust impulses, free to discover pleasures of erotic techniques she can't even imagine. But of course only invite her if you approve, my darling. There shall be no more Dominiques to disrupt our paradise.

Perhaps on second thought it's best we wait and see how she responds after this first visit before suggesting she reside longer; let's see how capable she is of applying herself with ease, grateful for the opportunity you are offering (you know how sulks unnerve me). But I sense in her eagerness to please. We shall see. Also her mons must not be waxed although you know I prefer yours to be—Phoebe's is another matter.

Until soon—my darling,
Talbot

"Get out get out get out!" Priscilla threw the letter at me and, screaming, ran from the room. I left it lying on the floor where it landed—a copy, of course—the original treasured next to my bed at Akeru, next to a photograph of Talbot. Then, having seen and done to my satisfaction all that I wanted to see and do, I said a pleasant good-bye to Phoebe as I passed her in the hall and marched out of Mrs. Talbot Bingham's Sutton Place house in New York City into my car, on to the airport, and off I jetted—home to Akeru.

BEE WAKES FROM THIS DREAM, remembering it in alarming detail. But in the afternoon falls into a deep sleep and, when she wakes, has no memory of it . . .

THROUGH COMPETENT SOURCES I have discovered that Maja's Janus Club is a five-story mansion on a quiet street in Brooklyn. Determined not to be found out to be an impostor, I arrive wearing sunglasses, confidently presenting myself as Bee. There appears to be a lot of bustle going on, but as I enter, someone runs to greet me, surprised. Obviously it is the flamboyant Maja who although distracted is delighted by my arrival, chatting on about the fête and Nadine who she says has been giving trouble lately and I've arrived just in time to take her down a peg or two. I tell Maja I miss Talbot, and, restless, left Akeru in charge of Rowena and staff for an indefinite time. As we talk it is clear to me she has no suspicion that my real identity is Priscilla, so I take off my sunglasses and look her in the eye as, smilingly, she looks back.

"Well, Bee, you haven't changed. Seeing you brings back happy times, and this is a most fortuitous visit—just in time for our annual Masked Fête tomorrow night. Come see how we are transforming the ballroom into a magic circle of a silver-and-crystal grotto."

Knowing nothing of the layout of the house, I hesitate: "I'll need something to wear—a dress, a mask; I forgot this is the time of year for the annual fête."

"Check with the atelier—they'll make up something for you in a jiff."

"No, let me first take a tour around to see if anything has changed since I left that night when Talbot came to claim me."

"Little has changed," Maja reassures me. "Our Janus Club is still best in the land—our goddesses make life their art. It's not easy to find ones up to your class or Nadine's, but I do have a new arrival ready to be presented in time for the fête—quite acceptable—Phoebe—she's learning fast. I've even found someone to replace Rowena, since you spirited her away from me. She's teaching a class right now in the Blue and Silver Room—as you're passing by take a look in. But oh Bee, we still all miss Talbot—so much—it's a credit to you that you kept The Rules he imposed to the letter and what a success you've made of Akeru! I congratulate you. And it appears you took my advice and preserved the deepest part of yourself intact—you did, didn't you?"

I turn away from her so she cannot see my tears.

"Never doubt he was genuinely admiring of you. Such a curious mixture, wasn't he—and, if you don't mind a bit of pop psychology from your ole *Mamacita*, I've come to the conclusion—a genius, yes—and to the world, a demigod, but as a man his desire to win honor, power, wealth, fame, and love of women came from lack of believing he had achieved enough of these satisfactions, and, like any other unsatisfied man, he turned away from reality and transferred his interests, and his libido too, into wishful constructions of a life of fantasy. But I must run, Bee," and she hurries off to attend to the fête.

I cautiously find my way around the house, imagining Talbot walking up the grand staircase, along these corridors, past rooms with doors closed. What has gone on here? What is going on there now? The front of each door is a painted trompe l'oeil, rendered so skillfully the figures appeared real. I reach out to touch the naked flesh, stunned to see each face resembles mine. Am *I* really here or am I too a dream?

As I turn to go down the staircase, someone in a great rush almost runs into me and seeing me, stops, exclaiming:

"Bee! What in heaven's name are *you* doing here?"

Stalling, to gather my wits I reply, "I got restless, missing Talbot—so I came back."

"Oh Bee, I've missed you—I'm on my way for a fitting but—come let's talk." And she pulls me to sit with her in an alcove on the staircase.

"Oh that lovely man—I'm sorry for your loss, Bee. No one like him, before or since, so generous to all of us, unlike any client I ever knew. I used to be so jealous of you, convinced it was me he should have chosen—I had the kind of moxie to cope with The Rules he required. I thought you much too romantic in the long pull to be ever able to hang in there. Anyone could see you were falling in love with him—I wasn't—which makes *all* the difference." Laughing, she rambled on.

"Remember, during the second half of the Yab-Yum when we each had a turn to display our skills at provoking his cock—I wasn't so sure—I thought he favored me. It's fair to say, Bee, even Maja puts me first in that skill. I'm eager to go for whatever it takes. Only when Talbot, turning me over, removed the balsa stick, replacing it with his cock, roughly, causing me to cry out—I didn't take to that one bit—so unlike him to cruelly comment I could never qualify as Maîtresse unless I be molded by the more severe golden rod.

"But later, Bee, when your turn came—

to my professional eye, you were much more interested in finding just the right size of a golden rod than in catering to his cock. I congratulate the time you took, considering the varying tapered sizes presented in the ebony box, intuitively selecting the one to please him. How inventive to suck it before inserting in you, leaving it there for a goodly time, sitting cross-legged to let him, without touching you, contemplate your beauty, and, after a time instructing you to remove it, bid me (not you, Bee) to pour aphrodisiac from the clay cruet into my hands, place a drop on my finger, lightly circle the tip of his cock, as you sat silently observing the pleasure I was giving him. But he never took his eyes off you Bee—don't think I didn't notice that! When the sweet musk scent filled the room he motioned me to give back the golden rod, knowing you would insert it with greater skill, but as he bent over the divan my tongue found its way to the secret crevices of his balls increasing his pleasure by taking his cock in my mouth as you rolled the rod gently around and up, higher into him with just the right edge. I learned a lot from you that evening, Bee. And he—enjoyed it mightily."

I am fainting, and taking her hand to steady myself, I blurt out, "Oh Nadine—I have to go now—no mask—have nothing to wear," and, about to ask directions to find the atelier, luckily I catch myself in time, for if I did she would discover I was an impostor. Flustered, astonished to hear myself say as she runs away from me down the stairs—

"It will be fun working with you again Nadine."

I look around the halls and finally come

upon the atelier where activity swirls in preparation for the fête. It stops when they see me standing in the doorway.

"Bee!" they all cry. "We missed you. Welcome home."

Later I learned that Maja encouraged members of the Janus Club to bring wives to her annual fête. I wondered if Talbot had ever in the beginning of our marriage even considered taking me? No doubt Maja knew from her discussions with him when he had enlisted her talents to find him a Maîtresse that I—his wife—was incapable of reciprocating passion in ways he required—knew I would not enjoy or condone the pleasures Janus provided. And, of course that was true. But now?

Priscilla couldn't believe it was her voice saying to Maja:

"Do you think Priscilla would have enjoyed coming with Talbot to Janus Club?"

"Hardly," Maja laughed. "I never met Mrs. Bingham, of course, but from everything I could gather she's a real uptight prude— totally unsuitable for Talbot. His genius had the creativity and the money to make Akeru and The Rules a reality. Not many of us can have our dreams come true in the way he did. Yes, his passions were excessive and obsessive indeed. He achieved everything he wanted, but I can't help but question sometimes—was it ever enough?"

"You mean—he *didn't* find what he was looking for at Akeru—The Rules?"

"Perhaps—perhaps . . ."

"How many wives do you expect at the fête?" I stand in the atelier as Maja supervises the fitting for my costume.

"Quite a few actually, the ones that do come are highly competitive. They have an uncanny way of zooming in on goddesses their husbands are, or have been, bewitched by. It's amusing to see how some suggest they retire with such a goddess to one of our private rooms, which, as you well know, are conducive to exploring all manner of pleasures. The favorite room still—you remember the one Talbot always requested—magenta satin walls, carpeted with red plush roses of velvet silk. Even I'm sometimes surprised when my goddesses tell me they've learned a thing or two from Wife, which is as it should be."

"Where does it lead?" my voice quavers.

"Often to behavior that wouldn't be tolerated anywhere except here."

"Is anything expected of me tonight?"

"No, Bee, just have a good time."

THE FÊTE HAS NOT BEGUN, but dressed and ready I wander restlessly to the fifth floor of the Janus Club and come upon a dark passageway leading to a door that has been left unpainted as though abandoned before the house was completed. Curiously, the door springs open as I approach and as if pushed by unseen hands I stagger into a room as brightly lit as an empty stage. As the door behind me shuts I know not if the room be big or small, as the walls and ceiling are mirrored. The floor is even coated with a silvery sheen, and although it is not made of mirror appears to be so. Dazed, I stand stunned as hitting and bouncing off the walls, back and forth, up and down, around, stretching into infinity, hundreds—no thousands—of images of a woman whose face is concealed by a mask of doves' wings and marabou feathers, her dress diamanté and woven with crystal stars, the tulle frothing around her like whipped cream. Closing my eyes, I twirl, willing the skin beneath this finery to shed like a chrysalis and when I open my eyes I will be Bee. Dizzy, I remove the mask—it is not Bee. It is I. Thousands of Priscillas crying out—*Yes, yes*—to the center of each of us—*she* for him, *he* for her—not me. What matter I be Wife? She will forever be his Queen.

In Santa Barbara, Bee on sudden impulse decides to surprise Maja by appearing unexpectedly at the Masked Fête. She throws her white dress sprinkled with diamanté and crystal stars into a suitcase, into it, too, the mask of marabou feathers and doves' wings Talbot placed across her eyes the night he brought her from Janus Club to Akeru. Her heart pounds as she looks from the window of the plane on its way to New York soaring into clouds and sunlight before rising into a nothingness of blue.

Dominated by mutual obsession, two eagles are now one. They travel, sweeping across mountains and valleys, oceans, deserts, toward each other, across forests by day, in dark of night, at incredible speed . . .

As midnight strikes, Bee appears at Janus Club.

Among the merrymakers a woman in a strapless tulle dress sparkling with diamanté and crystal stars, wearing a mask of white marabou feathers and doves' wings, mingles in the great hall as new arrivals push through the door.

Among them she sees a woman entering dressed as she is, wearing a mask of white feathers and doves' wings.

Simultaneously, the woman entering spots in the crowd another dressed as she is—and when she does—she falters—faints, but soon recovers.

She pushes through the crowd, tearing off her mask, moving swiftly toward the woman; she rips the mask off the other woman's face.

As this happens, the two women clasp their arms around each other.

And that, dear reader, is how obsession ends.